Mother Goose Rhymes

illustrated by CD Hullinger

Humpty Dumpty

Humpty Dumpty sat on a wall.
Humpty Dumpty had a great fall.

All the king's horses and all the king's men
Couldn't put Humpty together again!

Little
Miss Muffet

Little Miss Muffet
Sat on a tuffet
Eating her curds and whey.
Along came a spider,
Who sat down beside her
And frightened
Miss Muffet away.

Hickory, Dickory, Dock

Hickory, dickory, dock.
The mouse ran up the clock.
The clock struck one.
The mouse ran down!
Hickory, dickory, dock.

Jack and Jill

Jack and Jill
Went up the hill
To fetch a pail of water.

Jack fell down
And broke his crown,
And Jill came tumbling after.

There Was an Old Woman

There was an old woman who lived in a shoe.
She had so many children she didn't know
   what to do.
She gave them some broth without any bread.
She kissed them all gently and sent them to bed.

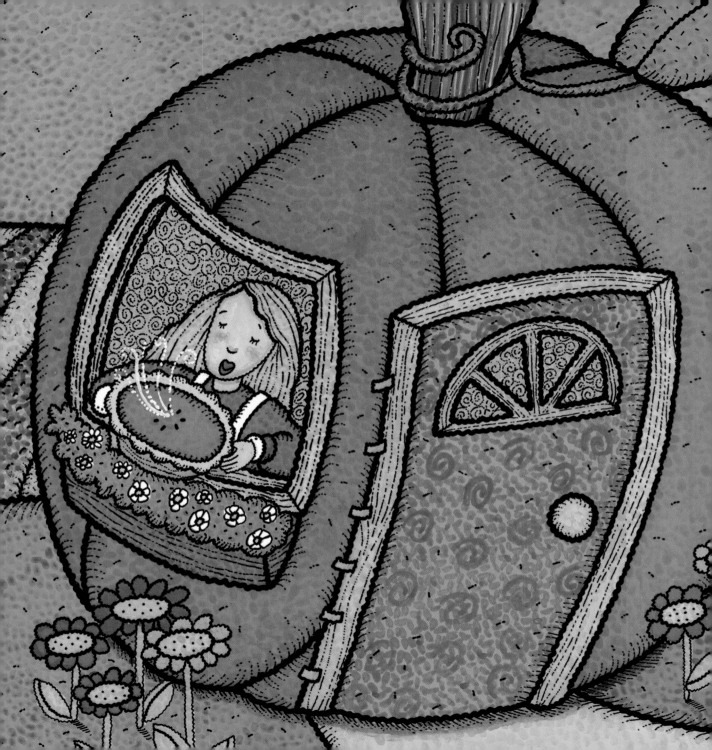

Peter, Peter, Pumpkin Eater

Peter, Peter, pumpkin eater,
Had a wife and couldn't keep her.
He put her in a pumpkin shell,
And there he kept her very well.

Twinkle, Twinkle, Little Star

Twinkle, twinkle, little star,
How I wonder what you are!
Up above the world so high,
Like a diamond in the sky.
Twinkle, twinkle, little star,
How I wonder what you are!

-Adapted by Jane Taylor

Baa, Baa, Black Sheep

Baa, baa, black sheep,
Have you any wool?
Yes, sir, yes, sir, three bags full.

One for my master,
One for my dame,
And one for the little boy
Who lives in the lane.

Baa, baa, black sheep,
Have you any wool?
Yes, sir, yes, sir, three bags full.

Hey, Diddle, Diddle

Hey, diddle, diddle,
The cat and the fiddle.
The cow jumped over the moon.
The little dog laughed
To see such sport,
And the dish ran away with the spoon.

To Market, To Market

To market, to market,
To buy a fat pig.
Home again, home again, jiggety jig.
To market, to market,
To buy a fat hog.
Home again, home again, jiggety jog.

Mary's Lamb

Mary had a little lamb,
Its fleece was white as snow;
And everywhere that Mary went,
The lamb was sure to go.
He followed her to school one day—
That was against the rule;
It made the children laugh and play
To see a lamb at school.

-Sarah Josepha Hale

Teddy Bear, Teddy Bear

Teddy bear, teddy bear,
Turn around.

Teddy bear, teddy bear,
Touch the ground.

Teddy bear, teddy bear,
Show your shoe.

Teddy bear, teddy bear,
That will do.

Teddy bear, teddy bear,
Run upstairs.

Teddy bear, teddy bear,
Say your prayers.

Teddy bear, teddy bear,
Turn out the light.

Teddy bear, teddy bear,
Say good night.

Little Jack Horner

Little Jack Horner
Sat in a corner,
Eating his Christmas pie.
He stuck in his thumb
And pulled out a plum
And said, "What a good
    boy am I!"

One, Two, Buckle My Shoe

One, two,
Buckle my shoe.

Three, four,
Shut the door.

Five, six,
Pick up sticks.

Seven, eight,
Lay them straight.

Nine, ten,
A good
fat hen.

Three Little Kittens

Three little kittens lost their mittens,
And they began to cry,
"Oh, mother, dear, we sadly fear
Our mittens we have lost."

"What! Lost your mittens?
You naughty kittens,
Then you shall have no pie.
Meow, meow,
Then you shall have no pie."

Three little kittens
Found their mittens,
And they began to cry,
"Oh, mother, dear,
See here, see here,
Our mittens we have found."

"What, found your mittens?
Then you're good kittens.
And you shall have some pie.
Purr-rr, purr-rr,
Then you shall have some pie."

Mary, Mary, Quite Contrary

Mary, Mary, quite contrary,
How does your garden grow?
With silver bells and cockleshells
And pretty maids all in a row.